Riding a Donkey Backwards

Wise and Foolish Tales of Mulla Nasruddin

retold by Sean Taylor
and the Khayaal Theatre

illustrated by Shirin Adl

CANDLEWICK PRESS

Contents

Meet Mulla Nasruddin

He has many names because stories about him are told in many different countries. In Turkey, he is Hodja. In Central Asia, he is Afandi. Others call him Mulla Nasruddin. He is a trickster, and Muslims all over the world love him because he makes them laugh.

If he doesn't make you laugh, he will certainly make you think—and perhaps think sideways instead of straight ahead. He may even make your thoughts do somersaults inside your mind!

Some say Nasruddin lived in the thirteenth century. Many different countries claim to be his birthplace, but nobody knows for sure when he was born, where he lived, or even if he was a real person.

Nasruddin is the wisest man in the village and also the biggest fool. He is sometimes an imam, a judge, or a teacher. He is often poor and usually hungry. But if he begs for money, he would rather take a silver coin than a gold one. If you want to know why, read on!

Sometimes Nasruddin can be seen carrying his front door on his back. Why? So that no one can enter his house while he's away, of course!

And he likes to ride his donkey backwards. Why does he do this? You will find out at the end of the book.

Whose Move?

One afternoon, a robber broke into Mulla Nasruddin's house. The robber stole everything he could carry. He took a carpet. He took the best cooking pot. He took a stool. He took the mulla's favorite cushion. Then he walked away.

Nasruddin came home just as the robber was leaving. The robber didn't see him. And Nasruddin decided not to shout or say anything. Instead, he followed the robber down the road. He followed him around the back of the teahouse. He followed him all the way to the other side of the village. Then, when the robber arrived at his own house, Nasruddin followed him inside.

As the robber put down the stolen things, Mulla Nasruddin got into a bed.

"What are you doing?" asked the robber.

"My wife and family will be joining us in the morning," Nasruddin told him. Then he pulled up a blanket. And he pretended to go to sleep.

"*What do you mean?*" asked the thief.

"Well," Nasruddin replied, "I thought we were moving to your house."

The Other Side

Mulla Nasruddin went fishing. The afternoon was warm. Everything was silent. And as he sat there, Nasruddin fell asleep.

He was snoring happily when a voice called out, "*Assalaamu alaykum*, Mulla Nasruddin!"

Nasruddin woke up with a jump. And he saw a man on the other riverbank, calling across to him.

"*Wa alaykum salaam*," said Nasruddin rather grumpily.

"Mulla," said the man, "please could you tell me how I get to the other side of the river?"

"What a birdbrain," muttered Nasruddin.
Then he called out, "You *are* on the other side!"

Drawing a Blank

One day, when Mulla Nasruddin was still a boy at school,
his teacher told the class to get out their pencils and draw a picture.
All the children settled down to draw.

Young Nasruddin was feeling rather tired, and he fell asleep.
Next thing he knew, the angry teacher was calling him up to
the front.

Nasruddin went, and the teacher asked to see
his picture. All Nasruddin had was a blank piece
of paper.

"Where's the picture?" asked the teacher.
"You didn't draw anything!"

"I did," said Nasruddin. "I drew a donkey eating grass."
"Well, where's the grass?" asked the teacher.
"The donkey ate it," said Nasruddin.
"And where's the donkey?" asked the teacher.
"There was no more grass," said Nasruddin.
"So the donkey left!"

The Traveler

One day, Mulla Nasruddin saw a man sitting by the roadside with a big, heavy bag. The man looked gloomy and tired.

"Why are you so unhappy?" Nasruddin asked.

"I'm on a journey to visit relatives," the man replied. "I hoped it would make me happy. But I still have a long way to go. This bag is so heavy. I'm tired. And I'm not happy at all!"

Without another word, Nasruddin grabbed the traveler's bag and ran off down the road, as fast as a rabbit!

The traveler jumped up. "No!" he called out. "THIS IS EVEN WORSE! NOW I'VE BEEN ROBBED!"

Around a bend in the road, the mulla saw a bush where he could hide.
He dropped the bag in the road. Then he waited behind the bush.

Soon, the traveler came up the road. He saw his bag and ran
toward it, smiling and dancing with joy. "My bag!" he cried.
"I've got it back! THIS IS WONDERFUL!"

Nasruddin came out from behind the bush. "You see?" he said.
"That cheered you up, didn't it!"

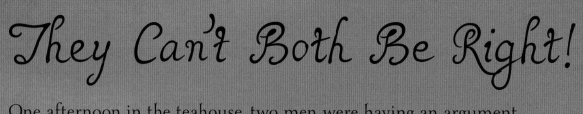

They Can't Both Be Right!

One afternoon in the teahouse, two men were having an argument. Nasruddin was sitting nearby. So they asked if he would decide which one of them was right.

Nasruddin listened as the first man explained his side of the argument. When he had finished, Nasruddin said, "You're right."

The second man called out, "No, Mulla Nasruddin! You must hear me!" And he told his side of the argument.

Nasruddin listened. Then he said to the second man, "You're right."

The owner of the teahouse had heard the whole conversation. He said, "Mulla Nasruddin! First you say one is right. Then you say the other is right. They can't both be right!"

Nasruddin put down his cup. He looked up and said, "You're right."

The Cooking Pot

Mulla Nasruddin went to a neighbor's house to borrow a cooking pot. The neighbor wasn't very happy about this. But she did agree to lend Nasruddin a big cooking pot.

The next day, Nasruddin returned the pot with a little pot inside it. "Your pot has had a baby," said Nasruddin.

The neighbor thought Nasruddin was crazy. But she was happy enough to take the new pot.

A week later, the mulla needed to borrow her pot again. Remembering the little pot she had been given last time, the neighbor was happy to lend the big cooking pot to Nasruddin.

The next day, the neighbor waited for Mulla Nasruddin to return her big pot. She was still waiting the day after that . . . and the day after that.

A week later, Nasruddin heard a knock on his door. It was the neighbor. "Nasruddin, where's my pot?" she asked.

"I'm so sorry to have to tell you this, but your pot died," said Nasruddin.

The neighbor became angry. "Don't be silly! How can a pot die?" she protested.

"Well," Nasruddin replied, "you were happy to believe a pot can give birth. So that must mean a pot can die!"

The Donkey Thieves

One day, Mulla Nasruddin bought a donkey in the marketplace. He started to walk home, leading the donkey on a rope behind him. But two thieves had been watching the mulla, and they followed him.

Without Nasruddin noticing, the thieves crept up behind the donkey. Then one of them took the rope off the animal's neck and put it around his own neck. Meanwhile, the other thief took the donkey back to the market to sell it.

The mulla didn't notice anything until he got home. When he turned around, instead of the donkey, there was a man standing behind him with a rope around his neck.

"Where's my donkey?" asked Nasruddin.

The thief went down on his knees. "Allah be praised, Mulla!" he said. "Thank you! You have broken a spell put on me. Because I was rude to my mother, I was turned into a donkey! I could only become myself again if a kind and generous master bought me. You must be the kind master! Now tell me what I can do for you in return."

"You can go back to your mother and apologize for being rude to her!" said Nasruddin.

So the crafty thief got up and ran back to his friend in the marketplace.

The next day, Mulla Nasruddin was in the market again, and he saw the very same donkey he had bought the day before. He went up to it.

Then he wagged his finger and said, "Naughty donkey! You've been rude to your mother again, haven't you?"

Silver or Gold?

Mulla Nasruddin had no money. So he went to the marketplace to beg for coins. He sat in the shade, near a shop owned by a rich carpet seller.

The carpet seller found it strange that Mulla Nasruddin, who was famous for being clever, was begging outside his shop. It made him wonder if the mulla was so clever after all. So he came up with a trick.

He went over to Nasruddin and held out two coins. "You can take whichever you want," he said. One was a small gold coin. The other was a silver coin, which was bigger but worth ten times less.

Nasruddin took the big silver coin.

The shopkeeper laughed because this was such a foolish thing to do.

The next day, he invited some friends to watch, and he repeated the trick.

Nasruddin took the big silver coin again!

Soon the whole town had heard this story. Lots of people offered a small gold coin and a big silver coin to Nasruddin. And they laughed when Nasruddin took the big silver coin.

A friend grew tired of seeing the mulla being laughed at. So he said to him, "Nasruddin, when they offer you two coins, you should choose the small gold one. It's worth ten times more than the big silver one."

"Thank you for your advice," replied Nasruddin, "but I don't agree. You see, if I choose the gold coin, everyone will stop giving me money!"

Do You Believe Me?

Nasruddin bought a handsome white donkey. He was very proud of it.

One day, there was a knock on the door. It was Nasruddin's neighbor. He wanted to borrow the new donkey to go on a journey over the mountains.

The mulla didn't much like this idea. He was worried his donkey would get injured on the rocky mountain trail.

"So, Mulla, will you let me borrow the donkey?" asked the neighbor.

Nasruddin shook his head. "I'm sorry," he said. "The donkey's not here. My son just rode to the market on it."

But at that moment, the donkey brayed loudly from the back of the house.

EEEE-AWWW!

Both men heard it clearly.

"It's not here?" said the neighbor. "But I just heard it!"

Nasruddin stared back. "What do you mean?" he asked.

The neighbor said, "That sound just now. That was your donkey braying!"

Nasruddin shook his head. "No," he said. "It wasn't."

"It *definitely* was," said the neighbor.

"Look," Nasruddin replied. "Do you believe me . . . or a donkey?"

The Sermon

Nasruddin was the imam at the village mosque. So every Friday, he gave a sermon.

One Friday, Nasruddin sat up on the pulpit. He looked at the congregation and said, "Do you know what I am going to tell you?"

"No," replied the villagers, "we don't know!"

"Well, if you don't know, what's the point of my telling you?" said Nasruddin. Then he left.

The next Friday, Nasruddin sat on the pulpit at the mosque again. He looked at the congregation and said, "Do you know what I'm going to tell you?"

The villagers remembered what had happened the week before. So they said, "*Yes*, we do!"

Nasruddin replied, "Well, if you know what I'm going to tell you, then what's the point of my saying it?" With that, he climbed down from the pulpit, leaving the congregation very confused.

On the next Friday, though, they were ready for him. Nasruddin sat on the pulpit and said, "Now, do you know what I am going to tell you?"

One half of the congregation said, "No."

The other half of the congregation said, "Yes."

"Good!" said Nasruddin. "Then those who know can tell those who don't know."

And he got down from the pulpit and went home.

Don't Ask Me!

Nasruddin was riding peacefully along on his donkey when it was startled by a snake on the path. The donkey jumped and began to gallop madly away.

Next thing he knew, Nasruddin was speeding past a field, and a young farmer called out, "Where are you going, Mulla Nasruddin?"

"Don't ask me!" Nasruddin called back. "Ask the donkey!"

A Nice Steam Bath

Nasruddin decided to visit the local hammam to have a nice steam bath and a massage.

A large man escorted the mulla into the hammam. But he didn't look after Nasruddin very well. The water was cold, the towel was small, and the massage was short.

Nasruddin wasn't happy. But as he was leaving, he gave the large man an extra ten coins. It was a very generous tip.

The following week, Nasruddin went to the hammam again. The large man was there, and as soon as he saw Nasruddin, he led him to the finest bath. He gave the mulla a big warm towel. He gave him a long massage with the most fragrant oils.

This time, Mulla Nasruddin was very satisfied, and as the mulla got ready to leave, the large man waited. He was expecting an even more generous tip. But Nasruddin left just one small coin. It was a very small tip.
The large man looked disappointed. So Nasruddin explained.
"This coin is for last week," he said. "And last week's coins are for this week."

Would It Be Possible for Me

A woman knocked on Mulla Nasruddin's door. "Mulla, dear neighbor," she said, "would it be possible for me to borrow your clothesline?"

"Let me ask my wife," replied Nasruddin, and he disappeared inside his house.

Very soon, he returned. "I'm sorry, dear neighbor," the mulla said. "But my wife cannot lend you our clothesline, because she has just sprinkled flour on it."

"Sprinkled flour on it!" exclaimed the neighbor. "Flour on a clothesline? What sort of person would do that?"

"The sort of person who doesn't want to lend it to a neighbor," said Nasruddin.

The Umbrella

A girl saw Mulla Nasruddin walking through the rain. He was carrying an umbrella, but he wasn't using it.

"Mulla!" called the girl. "It's raining! Why don't you use that umbrella?"

"It's broken," Nasruddin replied. "It's useless."

"Then why did you bring it with you?" asked the girl.

"Well," said Nasruddin, "I didn't think it was going to rain."

Tell Me One Thing

"Tell me one thing," said the mulla's wife to Nasruddin. "Why do you always answer one question with another question?"

Nasruddin gave a shrug and answered, "Do I?"

I've Lost My Donkey!

One day, Nasruddin came running into the marketplace. "I've lost my donkey!" he called. "Has anybody seen my donkey?"

One of the customers shook his head. Another said, "No. Sorry, Mulla Nasruddin. I haven't seen your donkey."

"Praise be to God! Praise be to God!" said Nasruddin.

Then the mulla ran to the school. "I've lost my donkey!" he called out. "Has anybody seen my donkey?"

A girl shook her head. A boy said, "No. I'm sorry, Mulla."

None of the children or the teachers had seen Nasruddin's donkey.

"Praise be to God! Thanks be to God!" said Nasruddin.

Then he ran into the mosque and he called out the same thing. "I've lost my donkey! Has anybody seen my donkey?"

The imam said, "I'm sorry, but I haven't seen your donkey, Nasruddin."

"Thanks be to God! Praise be to God the Beneficent and Merciful!" called out Nasruddin.

"Mulla Nasruddin," said the imam, "why are you thanking God *for losing your donkey?*"

"I am thanking God that I'm not on my donkey right now," Nasruddin replied, "or I would be lost as well!"

The Visitor

One day, an important imam arranged to visit Nasruddin at two o'clock in the afternoon. But when he arrived and knocked, the door didn't open.

Everything was silent. Nasruddin was not in.

After several minutes, the imam had had enough of waiting. He felt angry with the mulla. So he found a piece of chalk and wrote DONKEY BRAIN! on the door. Then he went away.

A while later, Mulla Nasruddin returned to his house, saw what was written on his door, and realized his mistake.

Right away, he hurried across the village to the important imam's house.

"Please forgive me for forgetting our appointment," he said. "I remembered about it as soon as I saw your name written on my door!"

Who Owns the Land?

An argument broke out between two farmers. There was a patch of land between their farms, and both men said it was theirs.

So they went to Nasruddin to try to find out who the real owner was.

Nasruddin went with them to the piece of land. The first man explained why the land belonged to him. The second man explained why the land belonged to *him*.

Then both the farmers looked at Nasruddin. "So, who does the land belong to?" they asked.

The mulla knelt down and put his ear to the ground.

The farmers stared at him.

Nasruddin looked up and he told them,

"The land says *you* belong to *it*."

A Cow up a Pole

Nasruddin managed to save some money. He kept it in a leather purse, and he wanted to find a safe place to hide it.

So he dug a hole in his garden and buried the purse there. But once that was done, he remembered that several strangers had gone past as he was digging. He grew worried that one of them might have guessed what he was doing.

So he dug up the money and brought it indoors. He thought about hiding it under the mattress. But that seemed rather obvious. He thought about leaving a note on the bed saying, "There is no money hidden under this mattress." But that seemed unlikely to work.

Finally, Nasruddin decided it would be best to stand a long pole in the ground and hide his purse at the very top of it. He was sure nobody would think there might be money hidden at the top of a pole.

But somebody did. A thief had seen what Nasruddin was up to. That night he crept into the mulla's garden. He climbed up the pole. He removed the purse and he stuck a lump of cow dung to the top of the pole.

A few weeks later, Nasruddin needed some of his money. So he took the pole down. And he found that his leather purse was gone. All that was up there was some brown cow dung!

Nasruddin scratched his head. He looked at the cow dung. Then he said, "How on earth did a cow manage to climb up a pole?"

When You Are Dead

One day, Nasruddin went for a walk with three friends. When they came to the cemetery, they saw a funeral procession arriving.

The first friend asked a question. "Imagine it was your own funeral," he said, "and your family and friends are all gathered around your dead body. What would you like to hear them say about you?"

The second friend replied, "I would like to hear someone say, *He was a doctor who saved many lives. And he was a good family man who loved his wife and children.*"

The third friend said, "I would like to hear someone say, *He was a hardworking teacher who inspired his students to love learning. And he was always honest.*"

Nasruddin stayed silent. So one of the others asked, "What would you like to hear people say about you, mulla?"

Nasruddin replied, "I'd like to hear someone say, *LOOK! HE'S MOVING!*"

What Are You Doing?

Mulla Nasruddin was sitting at the edge of a lake, spooning yogurt into the water.

A villager was passing by. He stopped to watch and asked, "What are you doing, Mulla?"

"I'm spooning yogurt into the lake," said Nasruddin.

"Why are you spooning yogurt into a lake?" asked the villager.

"It keeps tigers away," said Nasruddin.

"But, Mulla," replied the villager, "there are no tigers around here."

"I know," said Mulla Nasruddin with a smile. "It works well, doesn't it?"

So now you've met Mulla Nasruddin.
Remember that question at the start of the book?
"Nasruddin, why do you ride a donkey backwards?"

Glossary

Allah	God
Assalaamu alaykum	May the peace of God be with you.
congregation	A group of people gathered for a religious ceremony
hammam	A public bath where you can also have a massage
hodja	A Muslim faith leader (in Turkish)
imam	A Muslim prayer leader
mulla	A Muslim faith leader (in Arabic, Persian, Urdu, and other languages)
pulpit	A raised platform in a mosque or church from which a sermon is given
sermon	A speech containing religious teaching
Wa alaykum salaam	And may the peace of God be with you.

For the young writers at Harbinger Primary School
S. T.

For our grandchildren
E. M. and L. A.

For Kamyar and Dara
S. A.

With thanks to our helpers: Lynda Allen, Callam Berrah, Geoffrey Court,
Regina Machado, Abdullah Sadiq, Moniza Sadiq, Joey Taylor, and Rafa Taylor

With additional thanks to Mina Javaherbin, Moona Abdulkarim,
and the Malden Islamic Center in Malden, Massachusetts,
for their thoughtful support and assistance

First U.S. edition 2019
First published by Otter-Barry Books (U.K.) 2018
Library of Congress Catalog Card Number pending
ISBN 978-1-5362-0507-7

19 20 21 22 23 24 TLF 10 9 8 7 6 5 4 3 2 1

Printed in Dongguan, Guangdong, China

This book was typeset in Yana.
The illustrations were done in mixed media.

Candlewick Press
99 Dover Street
Somerville, Massachusetts 02144

visit us at www.candlewick.com